D0689754

Nadia Budde

BRISTLY HAIR
AND
I DON'T
CARE!

North
South

It isn't fair,
I have to say,

And
my burly
Uncle
Hurly,

thinks his curls
are far too curly.

Molly's little sister, Marge,

thinks her mouth's a bit too large.

Granny's purebred poodle, Dots,

would prefer a few less spots.

Our darling
kitty, Fluff,

hair she has,
just not enough.

Our neighbor Teddy Mounds

thinks he has
too many pounds.

And the boys,
if up to them,

would be just like supermen.

Some think if their
nothing else
Others feel
with butts too bouncy
Or maybe they
or bigger eyes
or shoulders like bricks
or necks as long
or muscles as big
or cheeks that glow
and cute little
or long and pointy
Parts they don't like

bellies were flatter
would ever matter.
they have it rough—
or not bouncy enough.
want puckier lips
or squarer hips
in a neatly stacked pile
as a country mile
as birthday balloons
like bright, full moons
round, button-like noses
one, just like a crow's is.
they want to be better...

...and so on and so on, etc., etc...

but my dear
Uncle Nooks...

doesn't care about looks.

...but the way you are

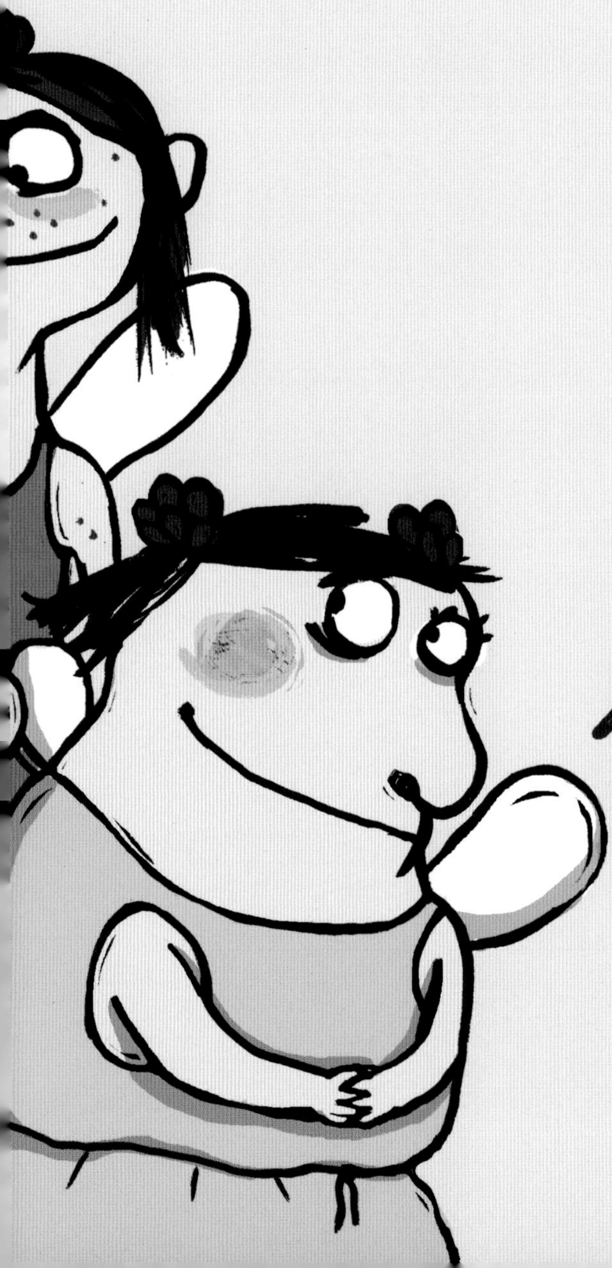

is the way that's right!"

Translated by Jeremy Frazkee

Copyright © 2013 by Peter Hammer Verlag GmbH Föhrenstr.
First published in Germany under the title *Und außerdem sind Borsten schön!*
English translation copyright © 2015 by NorthSouth Books, Inc., New York 10016.

First published in the United States, Great Britain, Canada, Australia, and
New Zealand in 2015 by NorthSouth Books, Inc., an imprint of NordSüd Verlag AG,
CH-8005 Zürich, Switzerland.

Distributed in the United States by NorthSouth Books, Inc., New York 10016.
Library of Congress Cataloging-in-Publication Data is available.

ISBN: 978-0-7358-4205-2
Printed in China by Leo Paper Products Ltd., Heshan, Guangdong, December 2014.
1 3 5 7 9 · 10 8 6 4 2

www.northsouth.com

Nadia Budde was born in Berlin, Germany in 1967. She studied graphic arts at the Berlin College of Art in Weissensee and later studied at the Royal College of Art in London. Her picture books have won numerous prizes and have been translated into multiple languages.